The Shoemaker's Dream

Masahiro Kasuya
Yoko Watari
English text by Mildred Schell

Judson Press ® Valley Forge

The Shoemaker's Dream

Original edition published in Japan by
Shiko Sha Company, Ltd., Tokyo, Japan 1980
© 1980 Masahiro Kasuya, illustrations
© 1980 Yoko Watari, original Japanese text
© 1982 Judson Press, English text by Mildred Schell
Based on "Where Love Is" by Leo Tolstoy
Published in the U.S.A. by Judson Press, Valley Forge, PA 19482-0851
Printed in Japan
Second printing, 1982
Third printing, 1984
Fourth printing, 1990
Fifth printing, 1996
ISBN 0-8170-0945-0
The name Judson Press is registered as a trademark in the U.S. Patent Office.

Once upon a time, in a tiny village in Russia,
there lived an old man whose name was Martin.
Martin lived in a basement apartment.
His home was also his workshop.

Martin was a shoemaker.
Every day he sat by his window and worked on
shoes. Sometimes Martin made new shoes
for the people who lived in his village. At other
times Martin carefully mended old
shoes and made them ready to wear again.

At the end of each day's work, Martin cleaned up his workbench and put away his tools. Then he cooked his supper and ate it, and washed the dishes.

After supper Martin lighted his lamp and took his Bible from the shelf. He opened the Bible and read about Jesus and how much Jesus loved all kinds of people.

One evening Martin was very tired.
He fell asleep while he was reading.
His head rested on the Bible.
Martin began to have a beautiful dream.
In his dream Martin believed that he heard
Jesus talking to him.
"Martin, my friend," said Jesus,
"tomorrow I am coming to visit you.
Watch for me in the street outside your window."

Then Martin woke up—and he was not sure
whether he had dreamed or not.
He shook his head and went to bed.
As he pulled the covers up under his chin,
Martin said, "Wouldn't it be wonderful if
Jesus really came to see me?"
He closed his eyes and went to sleep.
When he woke up, morning had come.

After breakfast Martin sat down at his window.
He looked up and down the street.
He hoped that he would see Jesus coming to visit him.
But all he saw was an old man in a thin coat.
The man was sweeping the snow away
from Martin's window. "How cold the poor fellow
looks," thought Martin.

Martin opened his door and called out to the man:
"Come, my friend," he said. "Come inside!
Warm yourself by my fire! Join me in a cup of tea!"
The old man looked surprised.
Then he laid down his snow shovel and hurried inside.

While the man warmed himself by the fire,
Martin made a fresh pot of tea and put brown bread
on the table. When the tea had brewed,
he poured two steaming cups—
one for his visitor and one for himself.
The two men sat down at the table.
They talked together as they ate and drank.

When the cups were empty and the last crumb had
been eaten, the old man said, "Thank you, Martin.
Your good tea has warmed my old bones.
Your good talk has warmed my heart.
I shall not mind the cold nearly so much now."

The old man left the warmth of
the room. He picked up his
snow shovel and went off down
the street.

Martin went back to his place by the window.
He looked up and down the empty street.
Then he picked up a ragged shoe and began to work.

Suddenly Martin heard crying sounds outside his window.
When he looked up, he saw a young mother with her baby.
The mother shivered, for her coat was not warm enough
for such a cold winter day. She held her baby close
to her so that the warmth from her body would
help to warm the child.

Martin dropped
his work and
rushed to the door.
"Young woman," he called.
"Come inside! Come
and warm yourself
and your baby."

Soon the mother and the baby were toasty warm.
The baby smiled and went to sleep.
The mother told Martin that the baby's father
was with the army in a faraway part of Russia.
She and the baby wanted to go there.
But it was so far away, and they
had no warm clothes.

Martin went to a chest in the corner of the room.
He opened a drawer and took out an old jacket.
It had been patched many times, but it was warm.
"Here," he said, as he handed it to the mother.
"Take this. It will help to keep you and the baby
warm. And may God go with you on your journey."

Tears came to the mother's eyes, but they
were happy tears.

"You are very kind," she said.
"My little one and I will never
forget the goodness of
Martin, the shoemaker."

She wrapped the baby in the
warm jacket and went on her way
down the street.

Outside Martin's window the snow fell softly.
Inside, Martin worked on his shoes.
As he worked, he thought, "It was such a lovely dream.
How I wish it might come true! How happy
I would be to have Jesus as my guest."
He sighed and went on with his work.

"You naughty boy! How dare you steal my apple!"
Martin dropped the shoe he was working on.
Outside his window an old woman held a boy by the arm.
In the boy's hand was an apple he had taken from
her basket. The boy tried to run away, but the old woman
held his arm tightly.

For the third time that day, Martin ran to his door.
"In the name of Jesus who loves little children,"
he called, "let the boy go. I will pay you for the apple!"
Then he turned to the boy. "You know it is wrong to
take things which do not belong to you.
Tell the lady how sorry you are!"

"I'm sorry, Lady," the boy said, looking up into her face.
The old woman let go of the boy's arm.
She nodded and smiled.
Then, as Martin watched, they went off down the street.
The boy was carrying the woman's heavy basket for her.
The old woman put her arm around the boy's
shoulders. As they turned the corner, Martin
heard them laugh together.

The day ended. Jesus had not come to
visit the shoemaker.
Sadly, Martin lighted his lamp and ate his supper.
Then, as he did every evening, he opened his Bible.
But it had been a busy day and Martin was tired.
He was soon fast asleep.
Again Martin dreamed that Jesus was speaking to him.
"Martin! Martin!" said Jesus,
"I came to see you today!
How much I enjoyed being your guest!"

Martin was puzzled.
"But, Lord," he said,
"I watched for you in the street all day,
and I never saw you.
When did you come?
Why didn't I know you?"

Then Martin's dream was filled with people.
First came the old woman and the boy.
"When you helped us settle our quarrel, Jesus was
with us," they said.

Next came the young mother
with her baby.
"When you gave us your jacket,
Jesus was with us," said the
mother.

Last came the old man with the snow shovel.
"When you took time to give me tea and to talk with me,
Jesus was with us," he said.

Then, as sometimes happens in dreams,
they
all
faded
out of
sight.

The old shoemaker woke up and rubbed his eyes.
He looked down at his open Bible and began to read:
   "I tell you, whenever you did this for one of the
   least important of these brothers of mine,
   you did it for me" *(Matthew 25:40, TEV).*

"Now I understand," whispered Martin.
He smiled, for he was the happiest man in
                the whole world.